Please return this book on or before the date shown above. To
renew go to www.essex.gov.uk/libraries, ring 0345 603 7628 or
go to any Essex library.

Essex County Council

Essex County Council

'Flight of the Dragons'
An original concept by Cath Jones
© Cath Jones

Illustrated by Michelle Simpson

Published by MAVERICK ARTS PUBLISHING LTD

Studio 11, City Business Centre, 6 Brighton Road,

Horsham, West Sussex, RH13 5BB

© Maverick Arts Publishing Limited February 2021

+44 (0)1403 256941

A CIP catalogue record for this book is available at the British Library.

ISBN 978-1-84886-765-9

www.maverickbooks.co.uk

This book is rated as: Purple Band (Guided Reading)

Flight of the Dragons

By **Cath Jones**

Illustrated by **Michelle Simpson**

Blaze and the other young dragons were very excited. Today was the day they would learn to fly! Their teacher was a dragon called Smokey. Blaze listened very carefully to her instructions. "Copy me and spread your wings as wide as you can," Smokey said. She stood on a large rock.

Blaze hopped on to a rock and spread out her wings.

"Now slowly flap," Smokey said. "Don't rush!"

Blaze and the other dragons flapped their wings up and down.

"Now, keep flapping and step off your rock."

Blaze flapped her wings and stepped off...

CRASH! She fell to the ground. All the other dragons whooshed up into the air.

"Wheee!" shrieked Little Leyla.

"Woo-hoo!" yelled Danoosh.

"This is so much fun!" cried Ember.

Blaze climbed back onto her rock. But each time she tried to fly, she crashed to the ground. She felt very sad.

"Why can't I fly?" she asked.

Smokey checked Blaze's wings. "Oh dear,"
she said. "Your wings are rather small."

"I was born with little wings," Blaze said.

Smokey shook her head sadly.

"I'm sorry, Blaze. Your wings are not big
enough for you to fly."

Blaze stared up at all her friends.

If she couldn't fly, how would she reach

Tanick Mountain? There was going to be a

big party on the mountain, to celebrate the

young dragons' first big flight.

She couldn't miss it.

The other dragons tried to cheer Blaze up.

"You have the best fire!" Little Leyla told Blaze.

"Your fire is brighter than any other," smiled Danoosh.

"Your fire is the hottest fire any dragon has ever breathed!" Ember cheered.

Smokey agreed. "You are a great dragon, Blaze. It doesn't matter that you can't fly."

But Blaze still felt sad. It was time to fly to Tanick Mountain and she couldn't go.

The dragons raced up the path and gathered

at the top of the hill. They raised their snouts

into the air. Tanick Mountain seemed to call

to them.

"Fly safely," said Smokey.

The adult dragons waved and wished them good luck. One by one, the young dragons spread their wings and tested the wind. Then they stepped off the hilltop. The wind took them, and they rose up into the air.

Blaze watched them soar and swoop in and out of the clouds.

"I wish I could fly too," she whispered.

Her friends circled the hilltop.

"See you soon, Blaze. Take care!" they called.

After a little while, the adult dragons set off on a different route to Tanick Mountain.

"Don't worry," said Smokey, "we'll be back soon." Then she took off too.

The elderly dragons stayed behind, but Blaze didn't want to wait with them. She moved to a different part of the hill and watched the last dragon vanish into the clouds.

Blaze was just about to set off back to her cave,

when she heard a strange sound.

Bang! Clank! Crash!

It was coming from behind an enormous boulder.

Blaze peered around the side. A strange heap of material lay on the ground. Next to it was a large basket and a girl was sitting beside it. She was crying.

"Are you okay?" asked Blaze.

"Oh!" said the girl, wiping the tears from her eyes. "I thought I was alone." She stared curiously at Blaze. "Why haven't you flown away with the other dragons?" she asked.

"I can't fly," said Blaze. "My wings are too small."

"Oh, I'm sorry," said the girl. "I can't fly either. I was going to try and fly with the dragons today, but my balloon is broken. I guess my family was right when they said it was impossible."

"Hmm, what's a balloon?" Blaze asked.

The girl smiled. "I'll show you. By the way, my name is Emma."

"I'm Blaze!"

"This was my balloon. I invented it so that I could fly with the dragons. I'd stand in this basket, then the burner would make fire and fill the balloon with heat. The heat would make it rise up into the air. Today was going to be my first flight, but my burner doesn't work. Without fire, I cannot fly," she said.

Blaze looked thoughtful. She took a

deep breath and blew a blast of fire.

Whoosh!

Emma gasped and clapped her hands

in delight.

"Maybe we could work together?"

Blaze suggested.

Blaze climbed into the basket, then Emma squeezed in beside her. It was just big enough for the two of them.

Blaze began to breathe fire into the balloon.

Soon, she had completely filled it with heat.

Now the basket lifted off the ground.

"Hold on tight," Emma shouted happily.

"We're off!"

Blaze gazed in wonder as they bobbed

through the air on a gentle breeze. She

loved the feel of the wind on her scales.

Whenever she felt the balloon stop rising:

Puff! She blasted fire.

Her fire carried them up into the clouds.

Blaze and Emma let out joyful shouts,

"We're flying!"

Blaze spotted something in the distance.

"Look!" Blaze cried. "Tanick Mountain!

Can we fly there?"

"I can't steer the balloon," said Emma.

"We have to go where the wind takes us."

"Perhaps I can try," Blaze said. She spread

her wings and tipped them to the side.

"It's working!" Emma gasped, as the balloon

slowly turned towards the mountain.

All of a sudden, there was a roar.

It was Little Leyla, Danoosh and Ember.

"Blaze, you're flying!" they cried happily.

They flew around the balloon in delight.

"Emma helped me! With her, I can fly!"

Blaze roared.

"And Blaze helped me! I'm finally flying

with dragons!" Emma shouted.

They were filled with excitement as they approached Tanick Mountain. Dozens of dragons were gathered there, ready to celebrate their successful flights. The adult dragons had prepared everything for the celebration.

As they touched down on top of the mountain, a triumphant roar filled the sky. Blaze had made it, and Emma was even made an honorary dragon!

From that day on, Blaze and Emma always flew together. They were the perfect team.

Quiz

1. Why can't Blaze fly?
a) She's too scared
b) Her tail is too big
c) Her wings are too small

2. Where do the young dragons fly to for their first big flight?
a) Tanick Mountain
b) Mount Everest
c) Cloudtop Mountain

3. What is Blaze good at?
a) Breathing fire
b) Breathing ice
c) Roaring

4. Why can't Emma fly?

a) The balloon is too small

b) The basket was broken

c) The burner doesn't work

5. How does Blaze steer the balloon?

a) Swishing her tail

b) Tipping her wings to the side

c) Blowing fire behind them

Turn over for answers

Book Bands for Guided Reading

The Institute of Education book banding system is a scale of colours that reflects the various levels of reading difficulty. The bands are assigned by taking into account the content, the language style, the layout and phonics. Word, phrase and sentence level work is also taken into consideration.

Maverick Early Readers are a bright, attractive range of books covering the pink to white bands. All of these books have been book banded for guided reading to the industry standard and edited by a leading educational consultant.

To view the whole Maverick Readers scheme, visit our website at www.maverickearlyreaders.com

Or scan the QR code above to view our scheme instantly!

Quiz Answers: 1c, 2a, 3a, 4c, 5b